This Puffin book belongs to

.........ferris ZACK Chapple

PUFFIN BOOKS
Published by the Penguin Group: London, New York, Australia,
Canada, India, Ireland, New Zealand and South Africa
Penguin Books Ltd, Registered Offices: 80 Strand, London WC2R 0RL, England

puffinbooks.com

Mr Biff the Boxer first published by Viking 1980
Published in Puffin Books 1980
Text copyright © Allan Ahlberg, 1980
Illustrations copyright © Janet Ahlberg, 1980

Mrs Vole the Vet first published by Viking 1996
Published in Puffin Books 1996
Text copyright © Allan Ahlberg, 1996
Illustrations copyright © Emma Chichester Clark, 1996

Miss Dirt the Dustman's Daughter first published by Viking 1996
Published in Puffin Books 1996
Text copyright © Allan Ahlberg, 1996
Illustrations copyright © Tony Ross, 1996

Master Bun the Bakers' Boy first published by Viking 1988
Published in Puffin Books 1988
Text copyright © Allan Ahlberg, 1988
Illustrations copyright © Fritz Wegner, 1988

This collection first published 2009
1 3 5 7 9 10 8 6 4 2

Made and printed in China

ISBN: 978-0-141-32682-5

Allan Ahlberg's

Happy Families Album

PUFFIN

Contents

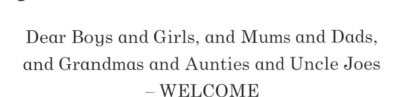

Dear Boys and Girls, and Mums and Dads,
and Grandmas and Aunties and Uncle Joes
– WELCOME
to Janet Ahlberg's, Emma Chichester Clark's,
Tony Ross's and Fritz Wegner's . . .

HAPPY FAMILIES ALBUM!

Oh, yes – and mine as well. Together the five of us
wrote and illustrated this book. And our Editor
edited it, and our Designer designed it, and our
HELPFUL AND WONDERFUL BOOKSELLER
put it in his or her shop for you to read
and YOU (yes, you) . . . bought it!

Hooray! And thank you all very very very much.

Now we're **all** happy.

Allan Ahlberg

Mr Biff
the Boxer

by Allan Ahlberg

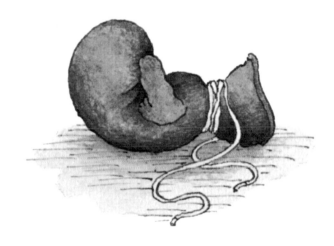

illustrated by
Janet Ahlberg

There was once a man named Mr Bop.

Mr Bop was a boxer.

He was as fit as a fiddle.

He was the toughest man in the town.

He was the champion.

There was another boxer in the town.

His name was Mr Biff.

Mr Biff was not as fit as a fiddle.
He ate too many cream cakes.
He drank too many bottles of beer.
Mr Biff was not tough.
He liked to sit in an easy chair
by a cosy fire.
He liked to put his slippers on
and read the paper.
He slept in a feather bed.

One day posters appeared in
the town. They said:

BIG CHARITY FIGHT

MR BIFF AGAINST MR BOP

Mr Biff told his wife
about the fight.
"It's for charity," he said.
"Me against Mr Bop."
"Oh dear," said Mrs Biff.
"They say he is the toughest man
in the town."
"They say his wife is the toughest
woman, too," said Mr Biff.

Mrs Biff told the children
about the fight.
"It's for charity," she said.
"Your dad against Mr Bop."
"Our dad will win," said Billy Biff.
"He will biff him!" Betty Biff said.

"But your dad is not fit,"
said Mrs Biff. "And he is not tough."
"We will be his trainers then,"
said Billy Biff.
"And toughen him up," Betty Biff said.
"You wait and see!"

The next day Mr Biff began training.

His family helped.

Billy Biff took him running.

Betty Biff took him skipping.

Mrs Biff hid his paper
and his slippers.
Bonzo Biff kept him out of
the easy chair.

The children also helped
to toughen him up.

Mrs Biff helped
to toughen him up too.

Mr Biff was put on a diet.
"I'd like three cream cakes
and a bottle of beer," he said.
"You can have three carrots
and a glass of water,"
said Mrs Biff.

Each day the children said,
"How do you feel, dad?"
Each day Mr Biff said,
"I feel terrible!"

But one day the children said,
"How do you feel, dad?"
And Mr Biff said,
"I feel as fit as a fiddle!"

Now it was the day of the fight.
A big tent was put up in the town.
Everybody was excited.
Crowds gathered.

The referee stepped into the ring.
"My lords, ladies and gentlemen,"
he said.
"On my right – Mr Bop!"
Everybody cheered.
"That's my husband!" said Mrs Bop.
"On my left – Mr Biff!"
Everybody cheered again.
"That's my dad!" Billy Biff shouted.

The time-keeper rang his bell.
"Ding-ding!"
The fight began.

Mr Biff stepped forward.

Mr Bop stepped forward.

Mr Bop moved to the right.

Mr Biff moved to the left.

Suddenly Mr Bop bopped Mr Biff.
At the same time Mr Biff biffed
Mr Bop.
They biffed and bopped each other out!

"It's a draw!" the referee said.
The time-keeper rang his bell.
"Ding-ding!"
The fight was ended.

In the dressing-room Mr Biff said,
"How do you feel?"
"I feel terrible!" said Mr Bop.
"I think bopping people is silly."
"Biffing people is silly too,"
said Mr Biff.
Then Mr Bop said,
"I feel hungry as well.
I have been on a diet."
"Me too," said Mr Biff.

"I could just eat a cream cake now!"
"And a jam tart!" said Mr Bop.
"And fish and chips!" said Mr Biff.
"And roast chicken and potatoes
and peas, and bread and butter,
and a bottle of beer!" Mr Bop said.

So that evening the two families
went out for a big dinner.
Mrs Biff made friends with Mrs Bop.
The Biff children made friends
with the Bop children.

Bonzo Biff shared a bone with
the Bop dog.
And a happy time was had by all.

The End

Mrs Vole
the Vet

by Allan Ahlberg

illustrated by
Emma Chichester Clark

Meet Mrs Vole the vet.
Mrs Vole has one son,
two daughters,
three cats,
four dogs
and *no* husband.

Mr Vole has three stepsons,
eleven rabbits
and a new wife.
We will forget about him.

Mrs Vole works hard.

She works day and night,

week after week

and all the year round.

No job is too little.

No job is too big.

No job is too fast,

too slow,

or too low.

. . . high.

No job is too . . .

Mrs Vole is worn out.
She comes home from work
and falls asleep in a chair.

Her children make the tea,
put her slippers on –
and worry about her.

"What you need is a *boyfriend*, Mum," they say.

"Hm," says Mrs Vole.

She sips her tea. "Do you think so?"

"Yes!"

"What sort of boyfriend?"

"A nice one!" the children yell.

"With a nice smile!"

"A nice wallet!"

"And nice football boots!"

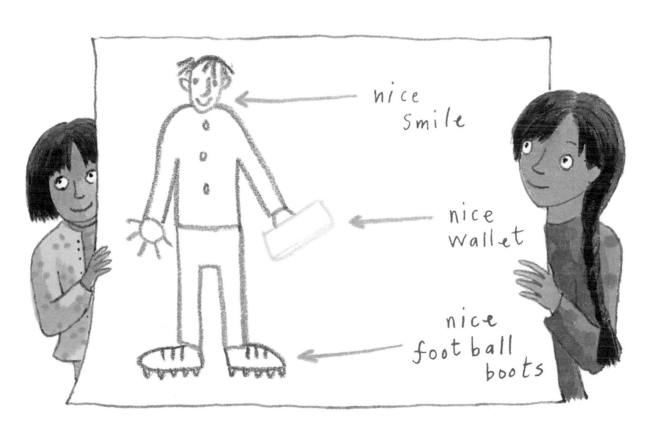

And Mrs Vole thinks, "Hm."

A few days later, Mrs Vole meets
Mr Lamp the lighthouse keeper.

Mr Lamp has a nice smile,
a nice cat
and a nice lighthouse.

"He's not bad, Mum," the children say.

"Hm," says Mrs Vole.

She sips her tea. "The only trouble is . . .

. . . TOO MANY STEPS!"

"OK," the children say.
"We will forget about him."

A few days later, Mrs Vole meets
Mr Field the farmer.

Mr Field has a nice smile, a nice truck,

 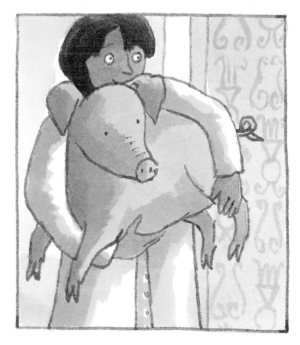

a very nice cheque book and a poorly pig.

"*He's* not bad, Mum," the children say.
"Hm," says Mrs Vole.
"Do you think so?"
"Yes!"

"Lovely cheque book!"
"Lovely pig!"
"Hm," says Mrs Vole.
She sips her tea. "The only trouble is . . .

. . . A HUNDRED AND FIFTY OTHER PIGS!"

"Phew!" the children say.
"We will forget about *him*."

Mrs Vole goes back to work.
She works seven days a week.
She works seven nights a week.

No job is too big.   No job is too little.

No job is too wet,

too spotty,

or too complicated.

No job is too rude.

Mrs Vole is worn out.
She comes home from work
and falls asleep at the table.
Her children make the breakfast,
put her slippers on –
and worry about her.

"What you *really* need
is a boyfriend, Mum," they say.
"Hm," says Mrs Vole.
She eats her cornflakes.
"Do you think so?"

A few weeks later, Mrs Vole meets:

Mr Shout the sergeant.
"Too bossy!"

Mr Green the grocer.
"Too cabbagy!"

Mr Aaargh! the actor.
"Too embarrassing!"

Aaargh!

"OK," the children say.
"We will forget about *them*."

Then, one morning the doorbell rings.
On the step stands a man
in a nice white coat.
He has a nice smile on his face
and a poorly pigeon in his hands.

Meet Mr Moo the milkman.
"Hallo, there!"

Mrs Vole takes care of the pigeon.
The children take care of the milkman.

When Mr Moo leaves,
the children rush up to their mum.
"*He's* not bad, Mum."
"Do you think so?"
"Yes!" the children yell.
"No steps!"
"No pigs!"
"No shouting!"
"You might be right," says Mrs Vole.
"The only trouble is . . .

. . . MRS MOO!"

A few days later,
Mrs Vole and the children
make a picnic
and drive off to the seaside.

The sun is shining.
The sand is warm.
The waves are splashing on the rocks.

Mrs Vole is smiling
as she climbs the *lighthouse* stairs.

"After all," she thinks.
"What's a few steps . . .

. . . between friends."

The End

Miss Dirt
the Dustman's Daughter

by Allan Ahlberg

illustrated by
Tony Ross

Daisy Dirt was an unusual girl.
She was the poorest
and the richest girl
in the whole town.

Daisy had lots to wear
and nothing to wear;
a huge room of her own
and a tiny room of her own.

She had a little dog

and a big dog,

a little hamster
and a big h . . . .

horse.

A big dinner . . .
and a *very* big dinner!

You see, Daisy lived
half the time with her dad
and half the time with her mum.

Daisy's dad was a dustman.
He was a divorced dustman on the dole.
"What's 'on the dole' mean, Dad?"
said Daisy.
" 'On the dole' means: out of work –
no money – skint!" her dad said.

Daisy's mum was a duchess.
She had got married again – to a duke.
He was a dozy duke in a Daimler.
"What's a 'Daimler', Mum?" said Daisy.

"This is!" said her mum.

Daisy's life was a whirl.
Here is her diary to prove it.

Monday:

~~breakfast with Dad~~
~~school~~
~~tea at Betty Biff's~~
~~house~~
home to Mum

Betty

Tuesday:

breakfast with Mum
school
tea at Maisie Maney's
house

home to Dad

And so on.
And so on.
And so on.

Yes, Daisy's life was a whirl.
She went back and forth
between her mum and dad
like a parcel –
like a pendulum –
like a ping-pong ball.

"I never know if I'm coming
or going," she said.

Then one day Daisy went
to her mum's and found . . .

nothing to wear,
nothing to eat —
and no horse!

There was a crowd in the street;
a car-boot sale on the lawn;
FOR SALE signs everywhere.

You see, the duke
had had some bad luck.
He was stony broke.

"What's 'stony broke' mean, Mum?"
said Daisy.
"'Stony broke' means: no money – skint!"
"Oh dear!" said Daisy.
"Yes," said her mum.
"I'm a down-and-out duchess."

But still Daisy's life was a whirl.
Still she went back and forth
between her mum and dad
like a homing pigeon
(with *two* homes) –

like a hamster in a wheel.

Here is her diary again to prove it.

Saturday:

breakfast with Mum
jumble sale with Mum
bike ride with Mum
home to Dad

Then one day Daisy went
to her dad's and found . . .

a crowd in the street;
a TV reporter at the door;
photographers everywhere.

You see, Daisy's dad
had had some *good* luck.
He had won the Lottery.

Then out they went for a drive . . .

. . . in a Daimler.

Daisy Dirt was an unusual girl.
She was the richest
and the poorest girl
in the whole town.

And she still is.

The End

Master Bun
the Bakers' Boy

by Allan Ahlberg

illustrated by
Fritz Wegner

Bertie Bun was born to be a baker.
His dad was a baker.
His mum was a baker.
His grandmas and grandpas were bakers.
His uncle was a boxer –
but that's another story.

When he was a baby, Bertie loved
to play with the flour and water.
When he was a little boy,
he loved to carry the bread.
But when he grew older, things changed.

One morning Bertie Bun
climbed out of bed,
came down for breakfast and said,
"I am browned off with bread –
and bored with baking."
"Oh, don't say that," said Mr Bun.
And Mrs Bun said, "Eat your toast!"

Later, Bertie went out
to deliver the bread.
On the way he met Billy Bone
the butcher's boy.
"I wish I was a butcher's boy,"
said Bertie. "Bread's boring."
"Let's swop, then," said Billy.
So they did.

But this only led to trouble.
Billy got lost with the bread,
and a bad dog ran off
with Bertie's sausages.

The dog belonged to Mr Creep the crook –
but that's another story.

Bertie came home for his lunch.

"I am very browned off with bread," he said.

"That's what you said this morning,"
said Mr Bun.

And Mrs Bun said, "Eat your sandwiches!"

In the afternoon Bertie delivered
the bread he should have delivered
in the morning.

On the way he met Barry Brush
the barber's boy.
"I wish I was a barber's boy,"
said Bertie. "Bread's boring."
"Let's swop then," said Barry.
So they did.
But this only led to more trouble.
Barry fell in the river with the bread,

and Mr Brush gave Bertie a free haircut
that he didn't really want.

Bertie came home for his tea.
"I am as browned off as ever with bread,"
he said.
"You're bald as well," said Mr Bun.
And Mrs Bun said,
"Eat your bread-and-butter pudding!"

Later that evening, Bertie played football,
had a bath and went to bed.

In the night he dreamt he was:

a bus-driver's boy

a bandleader's boy

a balloonist's boy

a bank-manager's boy

a bank-*robber*'s boy

a ballet-dancer's boy

and a bishop's boy.

He also had a bad dream
about loaves with little legs –
but that's another story.

The next day Bertie Bun
was still browned off with bread;
and the next day, and the next day,
and the next.
But the *next* day
Billy Bone came to tea.
"These sandwiches are good," he said.
"I wish my mum was a baker –
all I get is sausages."
And Bertie thought about this.

A few days later
Barry Brush came to tea.
"This bread-and-jam is beautiful," he said.
"I wish my dad was a baker –
all I get is haircuts."
And Bertie thought about *this*.

That evening Bertie watched
his mum and dad baking the bread.
He felt the heat from the ovens;
he smelled the hot-bread smell
in the air . . .
and was *not* bored.

The next morning Bertie Bun
climbed out of bed,
came down for breakfast and said,
"Bread's not so bad!"
"Hooray!" said Mr Bun.
"This son of ours is using his loaf."
"More toast, please!" said Bertie.
And Mrs Bun said, "Crumbs!"

Later, Bertie went out
to deliver the bread.
On the way he met Billy Bone
and Barry Brush –

and a performing dog.
The dog belonged to Mr Cosmo
the conjuror.
"I wish I was a conjuror's boy,"
said Bertie.
And Billy said . . .

... but, no.
What Billy said
and what Barry said
and what Bertie *did*, will have to wait.
There's no more room in the book.
And, besides, it really is ...

. . . another story.

The End

Please turn over . . .

. . . And so are these.
More Happy Families from the
long-running popular series.